The Porky Pig Counting Book

by Bernie Brosk
illustrated by Joe Messerli

MERRIGOLD PRESS • NEW YORK

Porky Pig has lots of deliveries to make today.

He delivers **one** bunch of flowers to Petunia Pig.

"Oh, thank you, Porky," says Petunia. "These flowers are just lovely. Did you remember the strawberries?"

Porky goes back to his bicycle and gets **two** boxes of strawberries. "Here you are, Petunia," he says.

"Thank you, Porky. They look delicious!" says Petunia.

At Elmer Fudd's house, Porky drops off **three** containers of ice cream.

"Elmer," says Porky, "why did you order so much ice cream?"

"I've got company coming," says Elmer.

Porky's next stop is Honey Bunny's house.
He brings Honey **four** rolls of crepe paper.
"What's the crepe paper for?" asks Porky.
"I've got a little decorating to do," answers
Honey.

Porky delivers **five** boxes of pretzels to Cicero Pig. "What are you going to do with all these pretzels?" asks Porky.

"I just love pretzels," answers Cicero. "Uncle Porky, where are the party hats I ordered?"

Porky Pig runs back to his bicycle. "Here they are. **Six** party hats. Are you giving a party?" asks Porky.

"No, but I'm going to one," answers Cicero.

Porky wonders whose party Cicero is going to.

Porky's last stop is Bugs Bunny's house.

"What's up, doc?" asks Bugs.

"Here are the **seven** party favors you ordered, Bugs," says Porky. "Are you going to the same party as Cicero?"

"Could be, doc," answers Bugs.

"And here are the **eight** bottles of carrot juice you wanted," says Porky. "Are you thirsty?"
"Yes," says Bugs, "I'm dying of thirst!"

"I almost forgot your balloons," says Porky. "Bugs, what are you going to do with **nine** balloons?"

"Come over to Elmer's house tonight at seven o'clock and I'll show you!" answers Bugs.

Porky Pig goes to Elmer's house at seven o'clock.

Can you guess why? It is Porky's birthday, and his friends are giving him a party!

There are **ten** presents on the table for Porky.

"Happy birthday!" everyone shouts.

"I forgot it was my birthday!" Porky says.

It is Porky Pig's happiest birthday ever!